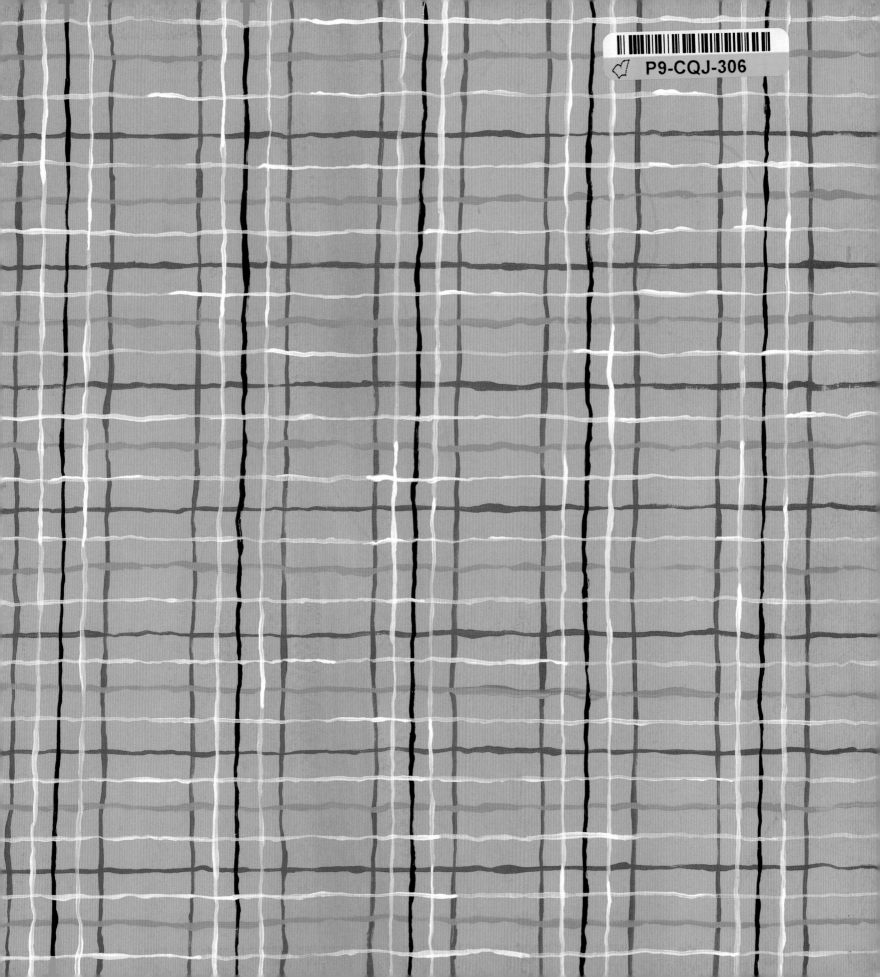

For Jack
and for Kara, fairy godmother, editor, friend
S. S.

For Cheryl, with love
P. M.

Text copyright © 2005 by Sarah Sullivan
Illustrations copyright © 2005 by Paul Meisel

First edition 2005

Library of Congress Cataloging-in-Publication Data is available.

Library of Congress Catalog Card Number pending.

ISBN 0-7636-2126-9

2 4 6 8 10 9 7 5 3 1

Printed in China

This book was typeset in Officina Serif.
The illustrations were done in mixed media.

Candlewick Press
2067 Massachusetts Avenue
Cambridge, Massachusetts 02140

visit us at www.candlewick.com

DEAR BABY
Letters from Your Big Brother

Sarah Sullivan   illustrated by Paul Meisel

CANDLEWICK PRESS
CAMBRIDGE, MASSACHUSETTS

Mom got you a rattle.

I got you a Stuffed animal.

December 3

Dear Baby,

Even though you will not be born for another three weeks, I've been thinking about you a lot and wondering what life will be like after you get here. Mom and Dad said writing you a letter might help me get ready to be a big brother.

I think I should warn you that there is not a lot of extra room in our house. Mom says there is plenty of room for a baby. I sure hope she's right.

Your brother,
Mike

Shoe Box

← your room (Ha, ha)

Dad got you this crib.

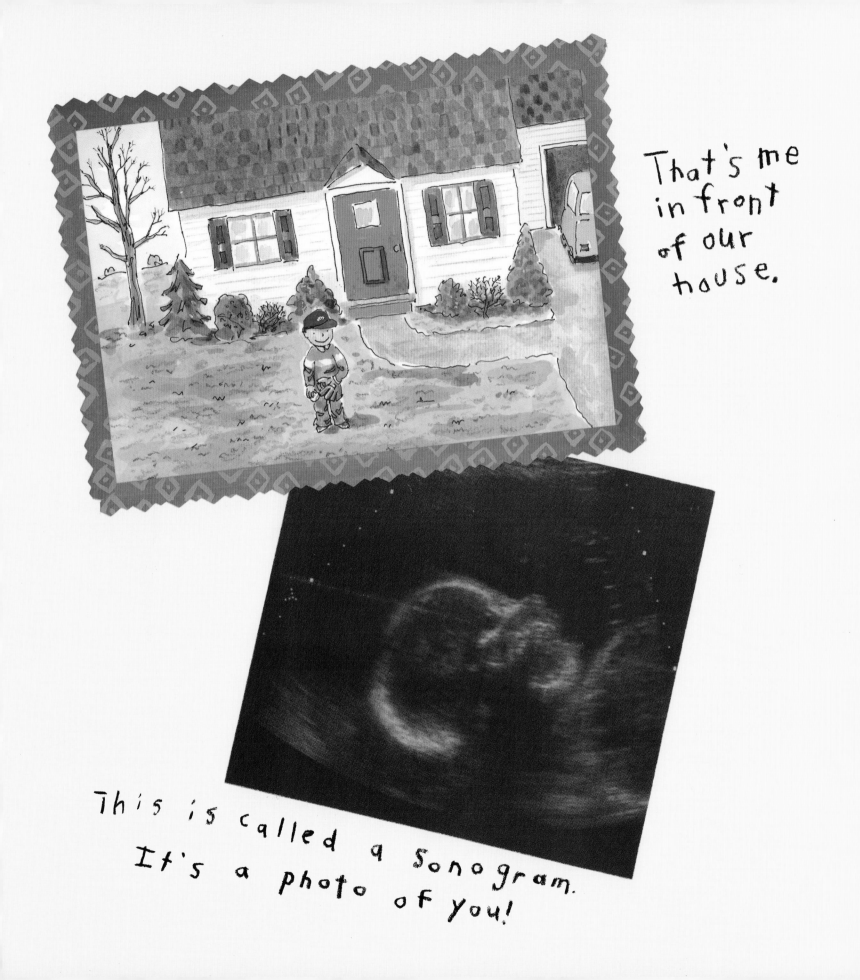

That's me in front of our house.

This is called a Sonogram. It's a photo of you!

December 16

Dear Baby,

Mom and Dad said it was OK to write you another letter. I want to let you know about something that is worrying me. I never had a brother or sister before. I'm not sure I know how. It would be nice if you are a boy because people will give you toys that I might like to play with. Also we can play soccer together when you get older. Dad says girls play soccer too. I hope you get here soon (I think).

Your brother,
Mike

My favorite toy—

Powerhouse
Mulligan

My team—
the Tornadoes
Yay!

me

January 2

Dear Baby,

   We are STILL waiting.
   Where are you?!!!

Your brother,
Mike

You sure can kick!

January 7

BABY GIRL

Dear Erica,

At last! You are born!
You came home from the hospital today. You have the tiniest hands and feet I have ever seen. And your face looks old and wrinkly. Mom and Dad think you are beautiful, but they also think asparagus tastes good, so you cannot always believe them.

Your brother (finally!),
Mike

WE ARE PROUD TO ANNOUNCE
THE BIRTH OF

Erica Louise

Born January 5
7 lbs, 6 ounces
19½ inches

We sent this out
to everyone
we know.

February 14

Dear Erica,

   Mom and Dad said it is OK for me to keep writing letters because someday you might like to read them.
   You are not so old and wrinkly-looking anymore. Now you look more like yourself, which is pretty cute, even if you do smell bad when you have a dirty diaper.

Your brother,
Mike

your stinky diaper

February 20

Dear Erica,

Guess what? My friend Rishi is going to have a baby brother or sister in about three months, so you are going to have someone to play with here on our street.

I'm sure Rishi will make a great brother, because he has a good friend to teach him what to do.

Your brother,
Mike

Me and Rishi

 How to take care of a baby brother or sister:

1. Don't eat their baby food.

Yuck.

2. Read them lots of books!

3. Make them laugh.

They like funny faces.

Grandpa and Grandma think you are sooooo cute.

→

March 14

Dear Erica,

I told Rishi he can come over and practice being a big brother ANYTIME HE WANTS! I also told him he is going to be sorry after the baby comes because nobody is going to care anymore what happens to him and he will be like the invisible boy in his house. He says he doesn't think it will be so terrible, but you and I know better, I think. Don't we?

Your brother,
Mike

Boo! Boo!

invisible!!

Boring
Baby ↓

Yucky
drool ↑

April 14

Dear Erica,

   I am getting tired of everybody always wanting to see you and hold you and talk to you all the time. What is so amazing about a baby who just lies there and blows spit bubbles with her mouth? I can do much better stuff than that, and nobody even notices I am here.

Your brother (who is practically invisible, thanks to you),
Mike

I can make better stuff than you.

May 2

Dear Erica,

Rishi got a new baby sister today. Her name is Maya, and Rishi's dad thinks she is beautiful. Rishi says she looks like a wrinkled-up string bean. I told him that is the way with babies. Parents are always thinking they are beautiful, no matter what they look like.

Your brother,
Mike

Things

french fries

Maya
by
Rishi

Rishi with his
parents and Maya

that babies shouldn't eat

my hand!

clam chowder

worms

toys

May 3

Dear Erica,

Rishi is going to stay at our house for a few days so his mom can rest and have plenty of energy to take care of the baby. We are having pizza for dinner, and Rishi says he wants to save a piece for Maya. Boy, does he have a lot to learn about babies! Who ever heard of a baby eating pizza? I guess it's up to you and me to teach him.

Your brother (who knows a lot about babies, thanks to you),
Mike

June 20

Dear Erica,

   No offense, but the way you eat your food is pretty disgusting! Maybe you could try keeping it in your mouth for a change instead of smearing it all over the table. I am only telling you this for your own good. Someday you are going to have to do it anyway.

Your brother,
Mike

Gross!

July 5

Dear Erica,

   You are six months old today, and Mom took you to the doctor for a checkup. I'll bet they gave you a shot.
   I'm glad you are my sister, but I'm wondering if you could learn to take longer naps so Mom and Dad will have more time to play with me.
   It's only a suggestion.

Your brother,
Mike

I thought you would never fall asleep.

Our picnic with Rishi's family

ERICA

August 12

Dear Erica,

Today I found a perfect woolly worm with fat black stripes. When I took it in the house to show Mom, she screamed, **"Don't get that near the baby! She'll put it in her mouth!"** She did not think my worm was beautiful. She only thinks you are beautiful. But you are a smelly dirty-diaper rodent, if you ask me. Not beautiful like a woolly worm. **Not even close!!**

Your brother,
Mike

a Snake

a butterfly

a woolly worm

IS **NOT** AS CUTE AS

r an ant

↳ a skunk

↳ a bat

Erica
by Mike

August 25

Dear Erica,

I'm sorry I called you a dirty-diaper rodent. Today was my birthday. You gave me a great present—a picture of you and me at the beach. Then you helped me blow out the candles. Now that I think about it, you're a whole lot better than a woolly worm, and your diapers don't bother me that much.

Your brother (who is one year older today),
Mike

We had a party in the backyard. →

For You, Grandson

You're Number 1!

← Grandma sent me a birthday card.

Some Things that you Will need When you go to School

Snacks →

↑ crayons

↑
money
for milk ↓

September 6

Dear Erica,

   School started today. Rishi and I are in the same class. Our teacher's name is Miss Park.
   Each kid in the class had to tell his name and something about his family. I said I have a little sister named Erica, who is real smart and who is a lot like me. Ha, ha.

Your brother,
Mike

Miss Park's
class

Do you
see
me?

a notebook ↘

↑ Lunch

↑
pencil with eraser

↑
a backpack

Look— you are almost walking!

September 27

Dear Erica,

I am getting a little mad at Rishi because he is always bragging about his sister. He says Maya is smarter than any other baby he knows. Just because she learned how to roll over does not mean she is smart. A dog can roll over. Big deal. You can do a whole lot smarter stuff than that! That's what I told Rishi.

Your brother,
Mike

WORLD'S SMARTEST BABY

A MEDAL I MADE for you

Best Baby Award

Maya can only crawl!!

October 10

Dear Erica,

Mom said I should apologize to Rishi. She says he is only being a good brother. She says I brag about you too, and Rishi doesn't get mad at me. I guess that's true.

Your brother,
Mike

BABY OF THE YEAR

P.S. When I apologized to Rishi, he said he was sorry too. Then I tried telling him that you are learning to walk, but first he wanted to tell me about Maya learning to crawl. Rishi's mom says that is the way with brothers. They are always thinking their little sisters are the smartest in the world.

October 25

Dear Miss No-Good Baby Sister,

This is **NOT** a friendly letter. This is a business letter. This is to tell you **NOT** to play with my toys **EVER** again!! Powerhouse Mulligan only has one arm now and **NO HEAD**, and we know whose fault that is, **DON'T WE?!!** You have plenty of toys of your own, so there is no reason to bother **MINE!!**

Your brother (who is looking for a new pen pal),
Mike

DO NOT TOUCH

NO BABIES ALLOWED

you have 3 boxes of your own toys!!

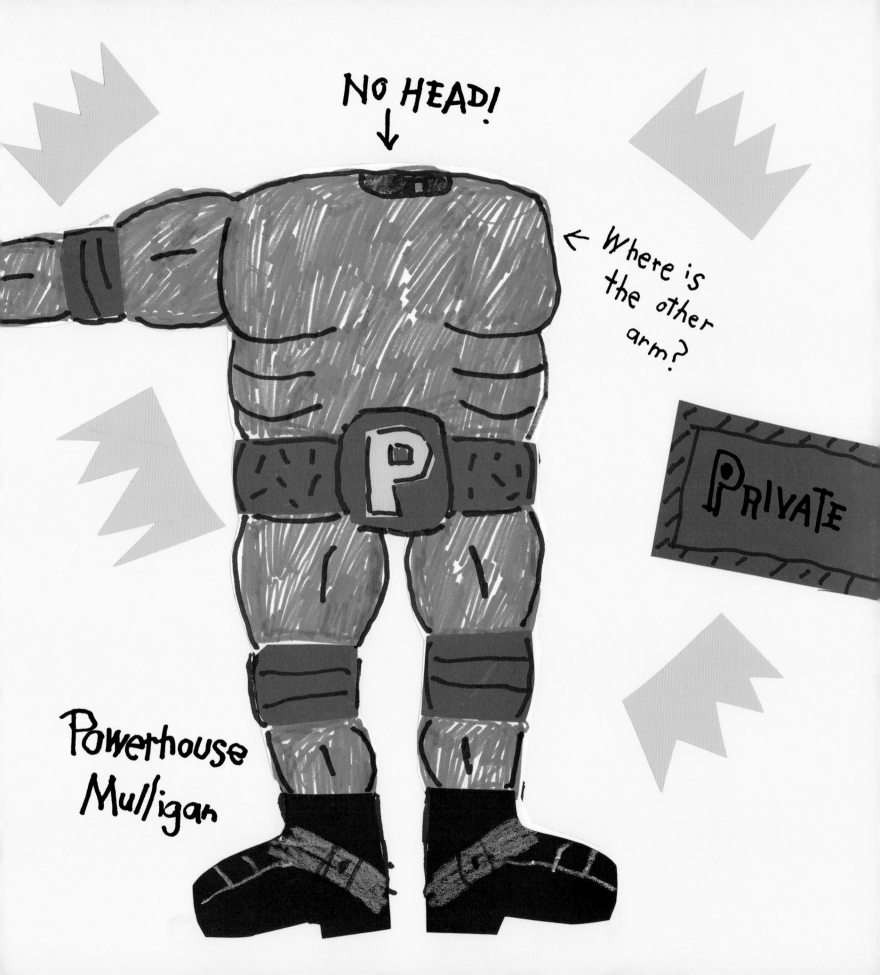

Rishi and Me

Boo

Maya and Erica

November 4

Dear Erica,

You were sick today and had a fever of 102. Your nose was runny and your eyes looked really sad. It made me feel bad, because sometimes I wish things were still the way they used to be before you were born, when I was the only kid in the family.

You are the best baby sister a boy could have! I hope you get well soon.

Your brother (who is sorry he ever got mad at you),
Mike

This is you when you were sick.

102!

Dear Erica

Get well soon!

I made this card for you.

November 23

Dear Erica,

Today is Thanksgiving. Grandma and Grandpa came for dinner. You ate mashed potatoes with gravy, sweet potato, beets, and a piece of pumpkin pie. Then you smeared cranberry sauce all over Grandma's shirt. Grandma said, "Look at Erica's finger painting, Mike. She's artistic, just like you!"

I have to remember to tell Rishi you're an artist too!

Your brother,
Mike

Things

←Mashed
potatoes

Your
first
Thanksgiving! →

you ate

cranberry
Sauce →

← pumpkin
pie

Sweet
potato
↓

beets

↑
your napkin

December 17

Dear Erica,

Today you nearly burned your hand on Mom's curling iron till I stopped you from grabbing it. Dad says part of being a big brother is helping you keep from hurting yourself. I never knew how much Mom and Dad would depend on me. It makes me feel important. Mom says it means I am growing up. I guess that's true.

Your brother,
Mike

If it weren't for me, you could fall off your changing table!

↑ You   Superbrother (me)↑   A monster↑

January 5

Dear Erica,

Today was your first birthday. You sure have changed a lot since Mom and Dad brought you home. At first I wasn't sure I was going to like having you around, but now I think having a little sister is the best thing that could happen to a boy like me.

HAPPY BIRTHDAY, BABY SISTER!!

Your brother (who loves you a lot),
Mike

Your party
↓

HAPPY BIRTHDAY

ERICA